WETLAND

by Sheila Rivera

first step nonfiction

Lerner Publications Company · Minneapolis

What is a **wetland?**

It is a place where water
covers the **soil.**

Some wetlands are near
lakes, rivers, or oceans.

Other wetlands are **swamps.**

A wetland is a kind of
habitat.

A habitat is where plants
and animals live.

Trees grow in some wetlands.

Grasses grow in some wetlands.

Moose live in wetlands.

Fish live in wetlands.

These beavers build a home
in a wetland.

Turtles live in wetlands.

Alligators live in wetlands.

Ducks swim in a wetland.

A frog eats an **insect.**

Many plants and animals
live in a wetland.

A Wetland Home

Many animals raise their young in wetlands. They hide among wetland plants to keep their babies safe from other animals.

Frogs, toads, and salamanders lay their eggs in wetland waters.

Thousands of different animals live in wetlands for all or part of their lives.

Wetland Facts

 Wetlands are found on every continent except Antarctica.

 Wetlands near the ocean are called coastal wetlands.

 Wetlands near lakes and rivers are called freshwater wetlands.

 Both water and land animals live in wetlands.

 Wetlands help clean streams and rivers by catching things that make the water dirty.

Wetlands help prevent flooding by holding extra water that overflows from streams and rivers.

 Some ocean animals live in coastal wetlands. Clams, crabs, shrimp, and fish live in some wetlands.

 May is American Wetlands Month.

Glossary

 habitat – where plants and animals live

 insect – an animal with three body parts and six legs. Many insects have wings.

 soil – the top layer of the earth

 swamps – pieces of land that are usually covered with water

 wetland – a place where water covers the soil

Index

The photographs in this book are reproduced through the courtesy of: © Tom and Pat Leeson, front cover, pp. 5, 7, 12, 13, 22 (second from bottom); © Kent & Donna Dannen, pp. 2, 9, 22 (bottom); © Karlene Schwartz, pp. 3, 22 (middle); © Bill Terry/Photo Network, p. 4; © Photodisc Royalty Free by Getty Images, pp. 6, 10, 14, 15, 17, 22 (top); © James P. Rowan, p. 8; © Arne Hodalic/CORBIS, p. 11; © Joe McDonald/CORBIS, pp. 16, 22 (second from top).

Illustration on page 18 by Laura Westlund.

Lerner Publications Company
A division of Lerner Publishing Group
241 First Avenue North
Minneapolis, MN 55401 U.S.A.

Website address: www.lernerbooks.com

Library of Congress Cataloging-in-Publication Data

Rivera, Sheila, 1970–
    Wetland / by Sheila Rivera.
        p.   cm. — (First step nonfiction)
    Includes index.
    ISBN: 0–8225–2598–4 (lib. bdg. : alk. paper)
    1. Wetlands—Juvenile literature. 2. Wetland animals—Juvenile literature. 3. Wetland plants—Juvenile literature. I. Title. II. Series.
QH87.3.R58 2005
578.768—dc22   2004020791

Manufactured in the United States of America
1 2 3 4 5 6 – DP – 10 09 08 07 06 05